Animal Stories

Animal Stories

by DICK KING-SMITH

Illustrated by Mike Terry

ORCHARD BOOKS   NEW YORK

First American edition 1998 published by Orchard Books
First published in Great Britain in 1997 by Viking/Puffin
"'Keep Yelling, Young Un'" was first published in Great Britain in 1983
by Victor Gollancz Ltd in *The Sheep-Pig* and in the U.S.A. in 1983 by
Crown Publishers, Inc., in *Babe: The Gallant Pig.* Copyright © 1983 by
Dick King-Smith. Published in 1985 by Puffin Books. Reprinted here by
kind permission of Victor Gollancz Ltd and Crown Publishers, Inc.

"Fat Lawrence" and "Woolly" copyright © 1997 by Fox Busters Ltd

"A Narrow Squeak," "The Happiest Woodlouse," and "The Excitement of Being
Ernest" were first published in 1993 by Viking in *A Narrow Squeak and Other
Animal Stories.* Copyright © 1993 by Fox Busters Ltd. Published in
1995 by Puffin Books.

"The Magic Crossing" was first published in 1987 by Hamish Hamilton Ltd
in *The Hodgeheg.* Copyright © 1987 by Dick King-Smith. Published in
1989 by Puffin Books.

"The Coronation" was first published in 1995 by Hamish Hamilton Ltd in
A Hodgeheg Story: King Max the Last. Copyright © 1995 by Fox
Busters Ltd. Published in 1996 by Puffin Books.

Illustrations copyright © 1996, 1997 by Michael Terry

Orchard Books
95 Madison Avenue
New York, NY 10016

Made and printed in England by The Bath Press
Electronic layout and composition by Helene Berinsky
1 3 5 7 9 10 8 6 4 2

The text of this book is set in 16 point Bembo.

Library of Congress Cataloging-in-Publication Data
King-Smith, Dick.
Animal stories / by Dick King-Smith ; illustrated by Michael Terry. — 1st American ed.
p. cm.
Summary: A collection of stories starring barnyard animals, including such characters
as Babe the pig, Lawrence the cat, and Ernest the cow dog.
ISBN 0-531-30099-4 (trade only)
1. Domestic animals—Juvenile fiction. 2. Children's stories, English.
[1. Domestic animals—Fiction. 2. Short stories.]
I. Terry, Michael, ill. II. Title.
PZ7.K616An 1998
[Fic]—dc21 97-51229

Contents

"Keep Yelling, Young Un"

from

THE SHEEP-PIG

Babe, the pig Farmer Hogget has won at the Village Fair, has been cared for by Fly, the sheepdog, and has made friends with Ma, the old ewe. To the amazement of both his friends, Babe has decided that he wants to be a sheep-pig.

Mrs. Hogget shook her head at least a dozen times.

"For the life of me, I can't see why you do let that pig run all over the place like you do, round and round the yard he do go, chasing my ducks about, shoving his nose into everything, shouldn't wonder but what he'll be out with you and Fly moving the sheep about afore long. Why dussen't you shut him up? He's running all his flesh off; he won't never be fit for Christmas—Easter more like. What d'you call him?"

"Just Pig," said Farmer Hogget.

A month had gone by since the Village Fair, a month in which a lot of interesting things had happened to Babe. The fact that perhaps most concerned his future, though he did not know it, was that Farmer Hogget had become fond of him. He liked to see the piglet pottering happily about the yard with Fly, keeping out of mischief, as far as he could tell, if you didn't count moving the ducks around. He did this now with a good deal of skill, the farmer noticed, even to the extent of being able, once, to separate the white ducks from the brown, though that must just have been a fluke. The more he thought of it, the less Farmer Hogget liked the idea of butchering Pig.

The other developments were in Babe's education. Despite herself, Fly found that she took pleasure and pride in teaching him the ways of the sheepdog, though she knew that, of course, he would never be fast enough to work sheep. Anyway, the boss would never let him try.

As for Ma, she was back with the flock, her foot healed,

her cough better. But all the time that she had been shut in the box, Babe had spent every moment that Fly was out of the stables chatting with the old ewe. Already he understood, in a way that Fly never could, the sheep's point of view. He longed to meet the flock, to be introduced. He thought it would be extremely interesting.

"Do you think I could, Ma?" he had said.

"Could what, young un?"

"Well, come and visit you, when you go back to your friends?"

"Oh ar. You could do, easy enough. You only got to go through the bottom gate and up the hill to the big field by the lane. Don't know what the farmer'd say though. Or that wolf."

Once Fly had slipped quietly in and found him perched on the straw stack.

"Babe!" she said sharply. "You're not talking to that stupid thing, are you?"

"Well, yes, Mom, I was."

"Save your breath, dear. It won't understand a word you say."

"Bah!" said Ma.

For a moment Babe was tempted to tell his foster
mother what he had in mind, but something told him to
keep quiet. Instead he made a plan. He would wait for two
things to happen. First, for Ma to rejoin the flock. And after
that, for market day, when both the boss and his wife would
be out of the way. Then he would go up the hill.

Toward the end of the very next week, the two things had
happened. Ma had been turned out, and a couple of days
after that Babe watched as Fly jumped into the back of the

Land Rover and it drove out of the yard and away.

Babe's were not the only eyes that watched its departure. At the top of the hill a cattle truck stood half hidden under a clump of trees at the side of the lane. As soon as the Land Rover had disappeared from sight along the road to the market town, a man jumped hurriedly out and opened the gate into the field. Another man backed the truck through the gateway.

Babe, meanwhile, was trotting excitedly up the hill to pay his visit to the flock. He came to the gate at the bottom of the field and squeezed under it. The field was steep and curved, and at first he could not see a single sheep. But then he heard a distant drumming of hooves, and suddenly the whole flock came galloping over the brow of the hill and down toward him. Around them ran two strange collies, lean silent dogs that seemed to flow effortlessly over the grass. From high above came the sound of a thin whistle, and in easy partnership the dogs swept around the sheep, and began to drive them back up the slope.

Despite himself, Babe was caught up in the press of jostling, bleating animals and was carried along with them.

Around him rose a chorus of panting, protesting voices, some shrill, some hoarse, some deep and guttural, but all saying the same thing.

"Wolf! Wolf!" cried the flock in dazed confusion.

Small by comparison and short in the leg, Babe soon fell behind the main body, and as they reached the top of the hill he found himself right at the back in company with an old sheep who cried "Wolf!" more loudly than any of the others.

"Ma!" he cried breathlessly. "It's you!"

Behind them one dog lay down at a whistle, and in front

the flock checked as the other dog steadied them. In the corner of the field, the tailgate and wings of the cattle truck filled the gateway, and the two men waited, sticks and arms outspread.

"Oh, hullo, young un," puffed the old sheep. "Fine day you chose to come, I'll say."

"What is it? What's happening? Who are these men?" asked Babe.

"Rustlers," said Ma. "They'm sheep rustlers."

"What do you mean?"

"Thieves, young un, that's what I do mean. Sheep stealers. We'll all be in this truck afore you can blink your eye."

"What can we do?"

"Do? Ain't nothing we can do, unless we can slip past theseyer wolf."

She made as if to escape, but the dog behind darted in, and she turned back.

Again one of the men whistled, and the dog pressed. Gradually, held against the headland of the field by the second dog and the men, the flock began to move forward. Already the leaders were nearing the tailgate of the truck.

"We'm beat," said Ma mournfully. "You run for it, young un." I will, thought Babe, but not the way you mean. Little as he was, suddenly he felt not fear but anger, furious anger that the boss's sheep were being stolen. My mom's not here to protect them so I must, he said to himself bravely, and he ran quickly round the hedge side of the flock and, jumping onto the bottom of the tailgate, turned to face them.

"Please!" he cried. "I beg you! Please don't come any farther. If you would be so kind, dear sensible sheep!"

His unexpected appearance had a number of immediate effects. The shock of being so politely addressed stopped the flock in its tracks, and the cries of "Wolf!" changed to murmurs of "In't he lovely!" and "Proper little gennulman!" Ma had told them something of her new friend, and now to see him in the flesh and to hear his well-chosen words released them from the dominance of the dogs. They began to fidget and look about for an escape route. This was opened for them when the men (cursing quietly, for above all things they were anxious to avoid too much noise) sent the flanking dog to drive the pig away and some of the sheep began to slip past them.

Next moment all was chaos. Angrily the dog ran at Babe, who scuttled away squealing at the top of his voice in a mixture of fright and fury. The men closed in on him, sticks raised. Desperately he shot between the legs of one, who fell with a crash, while the other, striking out madly, hit the rear-guard dog as it came to help, and sent it yowling. In half a minute the carefully planned raid was ruined, as the sheep scattered everywhere.

"Keep yelling, young un!" bawled Ma, as she ran beside

Babe. "The won't never stop here with that row going on!"

And suddenly all sorts of things began to happen as those deafening squeals rang out over the quiet countryside: birds flew startled from the trees, cows in nearby fields began to gallop about, dogs in distant farms to bark, passing motorists to stop and stare. In the farmhouse below, Mrs. Hogget heard the noise as she had on the day of the fair, but now it was infinitely louder, the most piercing, nerve-tingling, ear-shattering burglar alarm. She dialed 911 but then talked for

so long that, by the time a patrol car drove up the lane, the rustlers had long gone. Snarling at each other and their dogs, they had driven hurriedly away with not one single sheep to show for their pains.

"You won't never believe it!" cried Mrs. Hogget when her husband returned from market. "But we've had rustlers, just after you'd gone it were, come with a girt cattle truck they did, the police said, they seen the tire marks in the gateway,

13

and a chap in a car seen the truck go by in a hurry, and there's been a lot of it about, and he give the alarm, he did, kept screaming and shrieking enough to bust your eardrums, we should have lost every sheep on the place if 'tweren't for him, 'tis him we've got to thank."

"Who?" said Farmer Hogget.

"Him!" said his wife, pointing at Babe, who was telling Fly all about it. "Don't ask me how he got there or why he done it, all I knows is he saved our bacon and now I'm going to save his. He's staying with us just like another dog, don't care if he gets so big as a house, because if you think I'm going to stand by and see him butchered after what he done for us today, you've got another think coming, what d'you say to that?"

A slow smile spread over Farmer Hogget's long face.

Fat Lawrence

Cats come in roughly three sizes: skinny, middling, or fat. There is a fourth size—very fat.

But seldom do you see such a one as Lawrence Higgins. Lawrence was a cat of a fifth size—very, very fat indeed. He was black, and so big and heavy that his owner, Mrs. Higgins of Rosevale, Forest Street, Morchester, could not lift him even an inch from the ground.

"Oh, Lawrence Higgins!" she would say (she had named the cat after her late husband, even though he had actually been quite small and thin.) "Oh, Lawrence Higgins! Why are you so fat? It isn't as though I overfeed you. You only get one meal a day."

And this was true. At around eight o'clock in the morning, Lawrence would come into Rosevale through the cat flap, from wherever he'd been since the previous day, to receive his breakfast.

Then, when he had eaten the bowl of cat meat that Mrs. Higgins had put before him, he would hoist his black bulk into an armchair and sleep till midday. Then out he would go again—where to Mrs. Higgins never knew. She had become used to the fact that her cat only spent the mornings at Rosevale.

Five doors farther down Forest Street, at Hillview, Mr.

and Mrs. Norman also had a cat, a black cat, the fattest black cat you ever saw.

"Oh, Lawrence Norman!" Mrs. Norman would say (they knew his name was Lawrence; they'd read it on a tag attached to his collar, that day, months ago now, when he had suddenly appeared on their windowsill, mewing—at lunchtime, it was.) "Oh, Lawrence Norman! Why are you so fat?"

"It isn't as though you overfeed him," said Mr. Norman.

"No," said his wife. "He only gets one meal a day."

And this was true. At lunchtime, Mrs. Norman would hear Lawrence mewing and let him in and give him a bowl of cat meat.

Then, when he had eaten it, he would heave his black bulk onto the sofa and sleep till teatime. Then off he would go again—the Normans never knew where. They'd become accustomed to the fact that their cat only spent the afternoon at Hillview.

Round the corner, in the next street, Woodland Way, there lived at Number 33 an old man called Mr. Mason, alone save for his enormously fat black cat. It had slipped in through his back door one day months ago—at teatime it was—and he had read its name on its collar.

"Oh, Lawrence Mason!" he would say as, hearing that scratch on the back door, he let the black cat in and put down a bowl of cat meat. "Oh, Lawrence Mason! Why are you so fat? It isn't as if I overfeed you. I only give you this one meal a day and that's the truth."

When Lawrence Mason had emptied the bowl, he would stretch his black bulk out on the hearth rug and sleep till dinnertime. Then out he would go again—where to old Mr. Mason did not know. All he knew was that his cat only spent teatime at Number 33.

In front of Woodland Way was the park, and on the other

side of the park the houses were larger and posher. In one of them, the Gables, Pevensey Place, lived Colonel and Mrs. Barclay-Lloyd and their cat, who had arrived one evening at dinnertime, months ago now, wearing a collar with his name on it.

Mrs. Barclay-Lloyd had opened the front door of the Gables, and there, sitting at the top of the flight of steps that led up from the street, was this enormously fat black cat.

Each evening now, at dinnertime, the Barclay-Lloyds would set before Lawrence a dish of chicken nuggets and a saucer of Gold Top milk.

"Lawrence Barclay-Lloyd!" the Colonel would say. "I cannot understand why you are so fat."

"To look at him," his wife would say, "anyone would think he was getting four meals a day instead of just the one that we give him."

When Lawrence had eaten his chicken and drunk his milk, he would hump his black bulk up the stairs, clamber onto the foot of the Barclay-Lloyds' four-poster bed, and fall fast asleep.

The Colonel and his wife took to going to bed early, too,

knowing that at around seven o'clock next morning they would be awakened by their cat mewing loudly to be let out of the Gables. They never knew where he went, only that they would not see him again until the following evening.

For a long while, Lawrence was not only the fattest but also the happiest cat you can imagine. Assured of comfortable places to sleep and the certainty of four good square meals a day, he had not a care in the world.

But gradually, as time went on and he grew, would you believe it, even fatter, he began to feel that all this traveling—from Rosevale to Hillview, from Hillview to Number 33, from Number 33 to the Gables, and then back from the Gables all the way to Rosevale—was too much of a good thing. All that walking, now that his black bulk was so vast, was tiring. In addition, he suffered from indigestion.

One summer evening, while making his way from Woodland Way to Pevensey Place for dinner, he stopped at the edge of a small boating lake in the middle of the park.

As he bent his head to lap, he caught sight of his reflection in the water.

"Lawrence, my boy," he said. "You are carrying too much weight. You'd better do something about it. But what? I'll see what the boys say."

The "boys" were Lawrence's four particular friends. Each lived near one of his addresses.

Opposite Rosevale, on the other side of Forest Street, Fernmount was the home of a ginger tom called Bert, who of course knew the black cat as Lawrence Higgins. Next day after breakfast, Lawrence paid him a call.

"Bert," he said. "D'you think I'm carrying too much weight?"

"If you carry much more, Higgins, old pal," said Bert, "you'll break your blooming back. Mrs. Higgins must feed you well."

"She only gives me one meal a day," Lawrence said.

After lunch, he visited the second of the boys, who also lived on Forest Street, at Restholm, a couple of doors beyond Hillview. He was a tabby tom named Fred, who of course knew the black cat as Lawrence Norman.

"Fred," said Lawrence. "Tell me straight, tom to tom. Would you call me fat?"

"Norman, old chum," said Fred. "You are as fat as a pig. The Normans must shovel food into you."

"They only give me one meal a day," said Lawrence.

After tea, he waddled round the corner on to Woodland Way, where at Number 35 there lived a white tom called Percy. He, of course, knew the black cat as Lawrence Mason.

"Percy," said Lawrence. "Give me some advice. . . ."

Percy, like many white cats, was rather deaf.

"Give you some of my mice?" he said. "Not likely, Mason, old mate, you don't need any extra food, anyone can see that. You eat too much already."

"Do you think I should go on a diet?" asked Lawrence.

"Do I think you're going to die of it?" said Percy. "Yes, probably. Old Mason must be stuffing food into you."

"He only gives me one meal a day," said Lawrence loudly.

Percy heard this.

"One meal a week, Mason," he said. "That's all you need."

Later, Lawrence plodded across the park (being careful not to look at his reflection in the boating lake), and in Pevensey Place he called at the Cedars, which was opposite the Gables. Here lived the fourth of the boys, a blue Persian tom by the name of Darius.

Darius was not only extremely handsome, with his small, wide-set ears and his big, round eyes and his snub nose and his long, flowing blue coat; he was also much more intelligent than Bert or Fred or Percy.

"What's up, Barclay-Lloyd, old boy?" he said when he saw Lawrence. "You're puffing and blowing like a granddad.

You're going to have to do something about yourself, you know."

"The Colonel and his wife only feed me once a day," said Lawrence.

"I dare say," replied Darius. "But look here, Barclay-Lloyd, old boy, I wasn't born yesterday, you know. You're getting more than one meal a day, aren't you now?"

"Yes," said Lawrence.

"How many?"

"Four altogether."

"So at three other houses besides the Gables?"

"Yes."

"Bad show, Barclay-Lloyd," said Darius. "You'll have to cut down. If you don't, then, in my opinion, you're going to eat yourself to death. Just think how much better you'll feel if you lose some of that weight. You won't get so puffed, you'll be leaner and fitter, and your girlfriend will find you much more attractive."

"I haven't got a girlfriend, Darius," said Lawrence sadly.

"And why is that, Barclay-Lloyd, old boy?" said Darius. "Ask yourself why."

"Because I'm too fat?"

"Undoubtedly."

"A figure of fun, would you say?"

"Afraid so."

"Actually, girls do tend to giggle at me."

"Not surprised."

Lawrence took a deep breath. "All right," he said. "I'll do it, Darius. I'll go on a diet."

"Good show, Barclay-Lloyd," said Darius.

"I'll cut down to three meals a day," said Lawrence.

"One."

"Two?"

"One," said Darius firmly. "One good meal a day is all any cat needs."

For a little while, Lawrence sat, thinking.

Then he said, "But if I'm only to have one meal a day, I only need to go to one house."

"What's wrong with the Gables?" said Darius.

"Nothing," said Lawrence. "They give me chicken nuggets and Gold Top milk."

"What!" said Darius. "Well, you can cut the milk out, for

a start. Water for you from now on, old boy."

"But if I just stay here," said Lawrence, "the other people will be worried. They'll wonder where I've gone to—Mrs. Higgins and the Normans and old Mr. Mason. And I shan't see the other boys—Bert and Fred and Percy."

For a little while, Darius sat, thinking.

Then he said, "There are two ways to play this, Barclay-Lloyd. One is—you continue to make the rounds of your houses, but in each you only eat a quarter of what they put before you. Then that'll add up to one meal a day. Are you strong-minded enough to leave three-quarters of a bowlful at each meal?"

"No," said Lawrence.

"Then," said Darius, "the only thing to do is for you to spend the whole day at each house, in turn. And if you take my advice, you'll cut out breakfast, lunch, and tea. Stick to dinner. Which reminds me, it's time for mine. Cherrio, Barclay-Lloyd, old boy, and the best of luck with your diet."

To the surprise of the Colonel and his wife, that Sunday evening, Lawrence didn't touch his milk. He ate the chicken, certainly, greedily in fact, as though it was his last meal for some time, and he went to sleep on the foot of the four-poster as usual. But the next morning, no mewing roused the Barclay-Lloyds, and when they did wake, it was to find Lawrence still with them and apparently in no hurry to move.

On Monday, breakfast time came and went with no sign of Lawrence Higgins at Rosevale.

Lunchtime in Hillview passed without Lawrence Norman.

At Number 33, Lawrence Mason did not appear for tea.

Old Mr. Mason was worried about his black cat, as were

the Normans. So was Mrs. Higgins, but her worry ceased as Lawrence popped in through the cat flap at Rosevale that evening.

"Lawrence Higgins!" she cried. "Where *have* you been? You must be starving."

Lawrence would have agreed, could he have understood her words, and he polished off the bowl of cat meat that was put before him and hoisted his black bulk onto the armchair, and, much to Mrs. Higgins' surprise, spent the night there.

On Tuesday evening, Lawrence Norman appeared for dinner at Hillview.

On Wednesday evening, Lawrence Mason ate at Number 33.

Not until Thursday evening did Lawrence Barclay-Lloyd reappear for dinner at the Gables, much to the relief of the Colonel and his wife, who of course had not set eyes on their black cat since Sunday.

Gradually everyone grew used to this strange new state of affairs—that their black cat now only turned up every four days.

And gradually, as the weeks passed, Lawrence grew thinner.

The boys noticed this (though only one of them knew why).

"You on a diet, Higgins, old pal?" asked Bert.

"Sort of," said Lawrence.

"You're looking a lot fitter, Norman, old chum," said Fred.

"I feel it," said Lawrence.

To Percy he said, "I've lost some weight."

"What's that, Mason, old mate?" said Percy.

"I've lost some weight."

"Lost your plate?" said Percy.

"No, weight."

"Eh?"

"Weight!" shouted Lawrence.

"Why should I?" said Percy. "What am I waiting for?"

As for Darius, he was delighted that his plan for his friend was work-ing so well.

After months of dieting, Lawrence was positively slim.

"Jolly good show, Barclay-Lloyd, old boy," purred the Persian. "The girls will never be able to resist you."

"I don't know any."

"Well, between you and me and the gatepost," said Darius, "there's a little kitty living down at the other end of Pevensey Place. Tortoiseshell and white, she is. Dream of a figure. Amazing orange eyes. You'd make a grand pair."

So next morning, Lawrence woke the Barclay-Lloyds early, left the Gables, and made his way down Pevensey Place. I don't expect I shall like her, he thought. Darius was probably exaggerating. But when he caught sight of her,

lying in the sunshine on her front lawn, his heart leaped within his much less bulky body.

"Hullo," he said in a voice made gruff by embarrassment.

"Hullo," she replied in a voice like honey, and she opened wide her amazing orange eyes.

"I haven't seen you around before," she said. "What's your name?"

"Lawrence," muttered Lawrence.

"I'm Bella," she said.

Bella, thought Lawrence. What a beautiful name! And what a beautiful cat! It's love at first sight! It's now or never!

"Bella," he said. "Could we be . . . friends?"

Bella stood up and stretched her elegant tortoiseshell-and-white body.

"Friends, yes, I dare say," she replied. "But nothing more."

"Oh," said Lawrence. "You don't fancy me?"

"Frankly, Lawrence, no," said Bella. "I like the sound of you—you're nice, I'm sure—but you're much too slender for my taste. I've never cared for slim boys. I go for really well-covered types. As a matter of fact, there's a black cat farther up Pevensey Place—I haven't seen him about lately—but I really had a crush on him. Talk about fat, he was enormous! I do love a very, very fat cat, and he was the fattest!"

She sighed. "If only I could meet him again one day," she said.

You will! thought Lawrence. You will, and before very long too. And he padded away across the park to be in time for breakfast at Rosevale, followed by lunch at Hillview, tea at Number 33, and then back for dinner at the Gables, including a saucer of Gold Top and perhaps, if he could persuade the Barclay-Lloyds, second helpings. Oh Bella, he thought as he hurried along. You just wait!

A
Narrow
Squeak

"Do you realize," said Ethel, "that tomorrow is our Silver Wedding Anniversary?"

"So soon?" said Hedley in a surprised voice. "How time flies! Why, it seems like yesterday that we were married."

"Well, it isn't," said Ethel sharply. "You only have to look at me to see that."

Hedley looked at her.

She seems to have put on a great deal of weight, he thought. Not that she isn't still by far the most beautiful mouse in the world, of course, but there's a lot more of her now.

"You have certainly grown," he said tactfully.

"Grown?" snapped Ethel. "And whose fault is that, pray? Anyone would think you didn't know why I'm blown out like a balloon. Goodness knows what sort of a father you will make."

"A father?" said Hedley. "You mean . . . ?"

"Any time now," said Ethel. "And I'm starving, Hedley. Fetch us something nice to eat, do. I could just fancy something savory."

She sighed deeply as her husband hurried away. Was there ever such a mouse, she said to herself. So handsome, but so *thick*. Let's hope he doesn't walk straight down the cat's throat. I wouldn't put it past him, and then there won't be any Silver Wedding Anniversary.

A mouse's life is, of course, a short one, fraught with hazards. For those that survive their childhood, death looms in many shapes and forms, among them the cat, the poison bait, and the trap. Mice have learned to commemorate anni-

versaries in good time. "Better early than never" is a favorite mouse proverb, and Ethel and Hedley's Silver Wedding was to be celebrated twenty-five days after their marriage.

If they were lucky, they would go on to a Pearl, a Ruby, a Golden, and, should they be spared to enjoy roughly two months of wedded bliss, a Diamond Wedding Anniversary. Beyond that, no sensible mouse cared to think.

If only Hedley were more sensible, Ethel thought as she lay, uncomfortably on account of the pressure within her, in her nest. Not that he isn't still by far the most beautiful mouse in the world, of course, but he's so accident-prone.

Hardly a day passed that Ethel did not hear, somewhere about the house, a thin cry of alarm, indicating that Hedley had just had a narrow squeak.

He goes about in a dream, she said to herself. He doesn't *think*. Surely other mice didn't stand in the path of vacuum cleaners, or explore inside clothes dryers, or come close to drowning in a bowl of cat's milk.

In fact, Hedley was thinking quite hard as he emerged from the baseboard hole that was the entrance to their home and prepared to make his way across the kitchen floor.

"A father!" he murmured happily to himself. "I am to be a father! And soon! How many children will there be, I wonder?

How many will be boys, how many girls? And what shall we call them? What fun it will be choosing the names!"

This was what Ethel meant when she said that Hedley did not think. Her thoughts were very practical and filled with common sense, and she was quick to make up her mind. By contrast, Hedley was a daydreamer and much inclined to be absentminded when, as now, he was following up an idea.

He had just decided to call his eldest son Granville after a favorite uncle, when he bumped into something soft and furry, something that smelled, now that he came to think of it, distinctly unpleasant.

The cat, fast asleep in front of the stove, did not wake, but it twitched its tail.

With a shrill cry, Hedley ran for cover. The pantry door was ajar, and he slipped in and hid behind a box of corn-flakes.

The noise he made reached Ethel's ears and filled her mind, as so often during the previous twenty-four days, with thoughts of widowhood. It also woke the cat, who rose, stretched, and padded toward the pantry.

"Not in there, puss!" said its owner, coming into her kitchen, and shutting the pantry door.

Hedley was a prisoner.

For some time, he crouched motionless. As happened after such frights, his mind was a blank. But gradually his thoughts returned to those unborn children. The eldest girl—now, what was she to be called?

After a while, Hedley decided upon Dulcibel, his grandmother's name. But suppose Ethel did not agree? Thinking of Ethel reminded him of her last words. "Fetch us something nice to eat, do," she had said. "I could just fancy something savory."

Hedley raised his snout and sniffed.

This little room, in which he had never been before, certainly smelled of all kinds of food, and this reminded him that he was also a bit hungry. He began to explore the pantry, climbing up onto its shelves and running about to see what he could find. I'll have a snack, he said to himself, to keep me going, and then I'll find something really nice to take back to Ethel.

Much of the food in the pantry was in cans or boxes, but

Hedley found a slice of fruitcake, some butter in a dish, and a plate of chips. At last, feeling full, he hid behind a row of cans and settled down for a nap.

Meanwhile, back at the nest, Ethel was growing increasingly uneasy. He must have come to harm, she thought, and our children will be born fatherless. She was hungry, she

was uncomfortable, and she was more and more worried that Hedley had not returned.

"Oh, Hedley, how I shall miss you!" she breathed. "So handsome, but so *thick*."

While Hedley was sleeping off his huge meal, the pantry door was opened.

"Just look at this cake!" a woman's voice said. "And these leftover chips! And the butter—little footmarks all over it! We've got mice."

"Put the cat in there," said a man's voice.

"Can't do that or it'll be helping itself too."

"Well, set a trap then. And put some poison down."

And a little later, the pantry door was closed again.

Hedley slept the whole night through. He dreamed of happy times to come. In his dream, his handsome sons and his beautiful daughters had grown old enough to leave the nest, and he was taking them on a conducted tour of the house. Then boldly he led them all, Granville and Dulcibel and the rest, and their mother too, through the cat flap and out into the garden. "For we will picnic," he said to them, "in the strawberry bed. The fruit is ripe and the weather exceedingly pleasant."

"Oh, Papa!" the children cried. "What fun that will be!"

"But are you not afraid of the cat, Hedley dear?" said Ethel nervously.

"Ethel, Ethel," said Hedley. "When have you ever known me to be afraid of anything?" And the children chorused, "Oh, brave Papa!"

He woke from his dream with a number of other possible names in mind for the impending family—Eugene, Tallulah, Hereward, and Morwenna were four that he particularly fancied—when he suddenly remembered with a sharp pang of guilt that Ethel was still unfed.

I shall get the rough edge of her tongue, he thought, and he looked about for a tasty item of food small enough for him to carry.

He climbed down to a lower shelf and found something that had not, he was sure, been there before.

It was a saucer containing a number of little blue pellets, and beside it there was an opened box. Had Hedley been able to read, he would have seen that on the box was written:

MOUSE POISON,

KEEP AWAY FROM DOMESTIC ANIMALS

As it was, thinking how unusual and attractive the blue pellets looked, he took a mouthful of them. She'll love these, he thought, such a pretty color. And he ran down to the floor of the pantry, only to find the door shut. Bother, thought Hedley. How am I to get out of this place?

He was considering this problem in a halfhearted way, for part of his mind was still occupied with names—would Annabel be better than Morwenna?—when his nose caught a most exciting smell. It was cheese, a little square lump of it, conveniently placed on a low shelf.

The cheese was, in fact, on a little wooden platform, an odd-looking thing that had a metal arm and a spring attached to it. But Hedley, busy deciding that, after all, he preferred Morwenna, did not stop to think about this. It's Ethel's favorite food, he said to himself, and just the right

size for me to carry back, and he spit out the little blue pellets and ran to grab the cheese.

Whether it was his speed or whether the trap had not
been properly set, Hedley got away with it.

Snap! went the trap, missing him (though not by a whisker, for it cut off three of them), and Hedley gave a muffled squeak of fright through his mouthful of cheese.

"Listen!" said the woman's voice, and "You got him!" said the man's, and the pantry door was opened.

For once, Hedley did not daydream. He streaked across the kitchen floor and into his hole, the lump of cheese clenched in his jaws.

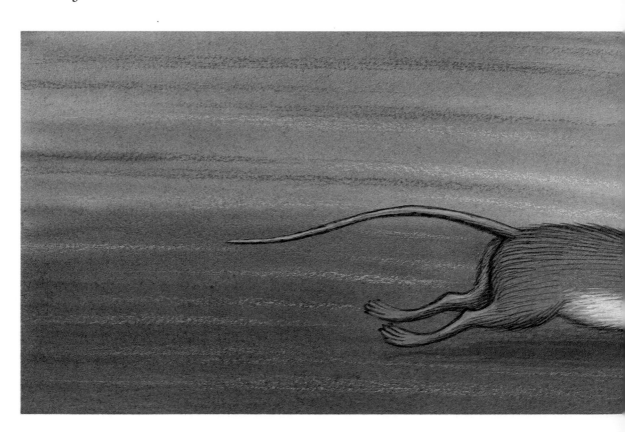

Ethel regarded him silently from the nest.

Hedley dropped his burden before her.

"Sorry I'm late," he panted. "I got held up. Here, it's farmhouse cheddar, your favorite. How have you been?"

"Busy," said Ethel shortly.

"Busy?" said Hedley.

"Yes," said Ethel.

She attacked the cheese hungrily, while Hedley got his breath back. Funny, he thought, she looks slimmer than she

did yesterday. As slim, in fact, as the day we met, and what a meeting that was! I remember it as though it were yesterday. . . .

"Hedley!" said Ethel now, licking her lips as she finished the cheese. "You do know what day it is, don't you?"

"Wednesday, I think," said Hedley. "Or it may be Thursday. I'm not sure."

"Hedley," said Ethel. "It is our Silver Wedding Anniversary."

"Oh!" cried Hedley. "I quite forgot."

Typical, thought Ethel. He'd forget his head if it weren't screwed on.

"I have a present for you," she said, and she rose and stood back from the nest.

In the middle of a comfortable, warm bed, made out of flock from a chair lining, feathers from an eiderdown, and a mass of newspaper scraps, lay six fat, pink, naked babies.

"Three boys and three girls," she said. "Neat, eh?"

Oh! thought Hedley. What could be neater! Granville and Dulcibel, Eugene and Tallulah, and Hereward and Morwenna.

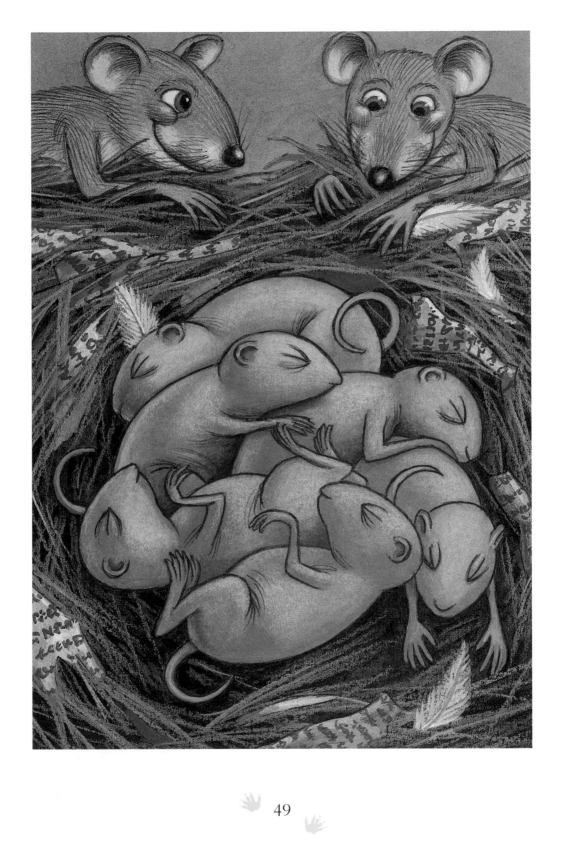

"Oh, Ethel dearest," he said. "I have no present for you but my love."

At these words, Ethel's annoyance melted away. What a fine-looking mouse he still is, she thought, not a gray hair on him. In fact, he looks no older than he did at our wedding, twenty-five long days ago.

Hedley sat in a daze, gazing at the babies.

Then he said, "Oh, Ethel! To think that you did this all on your own! You're so *clever!*"

And you're so *thick,* thought Ethel fondly, but out loud she said, "Oh, Hedley, you are *so* handsome!"

The Magic Crossing

from

THE HODGEHEG

Max the hedgehog is trying to discover a safe way for hedgehogs
to cross the road. In doing so, he bangs his head, and now
everything he says comes out backward. But Max is undaunted.

That evening, Max waited until he was sure that Pa was out of the way, in the garden of Number 5B. The people in 5A always put out bread and milk for Max's family, but the people in 5B often provided something much better for their hedgehogs—canned dog food.

Every evening, Pa crept through the

dividing hedge to see if he could steal a saucerful of Munchimeat before his neighbor woke from the day's sleep.

"Ma," said Max, "I'm walking for a go."

Ma was quick at translating by now.

"Did Pa say you could go?" she said.

"No," said Max, "but he couldn't say I didn't." And before Ma could do anything, he trotted off along the garden path.

"Oh, Max!" called Ma. "Are you sure you'll be all right?"

"Yes, of course," said Max. "I'll be quite KO."

Once outside the garden gate, he turned left and set off up the road, in the opposite direction from his previous effort. By now, he was used to the noise and the brightness, and confident that he was safe from traffic as long as he did not step down into the road. When a human passed, he stood still. The creatures did not notice you, he found, if you did not move.

He trotted on, past the garden of Number 9A with its widow and six kids, until the row of houses ended and a high factory wall began, so high that he would not have been able to read the notice on it beside the factory

53

entrance: Max Speed 5 M.P.H. it said.

Max kept going (a good deal more slowly than this), and then suddenly, once again, he saw, not far ahead, what he was seeking. Again there were people crossing the street!

This time, they did not go in ones and twos at random, but waited all together and then, at some signal, he supposed, crossed at the same time. Max drew nearer, until he could hear at intervals a high rapid peep-peep-peeping noise, at the sound of which the traffic stopped and the people walked across in safety.

Creeping closer still, tight up against the wall, he finally reached the crossing, and now he could see this new magic method. The bunch of humans stood and watched, just above their heads, a picture of a little red man standing quite still. The people stood quite still. Then suddenly the little red man disappeared, and underneath him there was a picture of a little green man, walking, swinging his arms. The people walked, swinging their arms, while the high rapid peep-peep-peeping noise warned the traffic not to move.

Max sat and watched for quite a long time, fascinated by the red man and the green man. He rather wished they could have been a red hedgehog and a green hedgehog, but that was not really important, as long as hedgehogs could cross here safely. That was all he had to prove, and the sooner the better.

He edged forward, until he was just behind the waiting humans, and watched tensely for the little green man to walk.

What Max had not bargained for, when the bunch of people moved off at the peep-peep-peeping of the little green man, was that another bunch would be coming toward him

from the other side of the street. So when he was about halfway across, hurrying along at the heels of one crowd, he was suddenly confronted by another. He dodged about in a forest of legs, in great danger of being stepped on. No one seemed to notice his small shape, and indeed, he was kicked by a large foot and he rolled backward.

Picking himself up, he looked across and found, to his horror, that the green man was gone and the red man had reappeared. Frantically Max ran on, as the traffic began to move, and reached the far side inches in front of a great wheel that almost brushed his backside. The shock of so narrow an escape made him roll up. And for some time, he lay in the gutter while above his head the humans stepped onto or off the pavement and the noisy green man and the silent red man lit up in turn.

After a while, there seemed to be fewer people about, and Max uncurled and climbed over the curb. He turned right and set off in the direction of home. How to recross the street was something he had not yet worked out, but in his experience, neither a crosswalk nor red and green men were the answer.

As usual, he kept close to the wall at the inner edge of the pavement, a wall that presently gave way to iron railings. These were wide enough apart for even the largest hedgehog to pass between. Max slipped through. In the light of a full moon, he could see before him a wide stretch of grass, and he ran across it until the noise and stink of the traffic were left behind.

"Am I where?" said Max, looking around him. His nose told him of the scent of flowers (in the ornamental gardens), his eyes told him of a strangely shaped building (the bandstand), and his ears told him of the sound of splashing water (as the fountain spouted endlessly in the lily pond).

Of course! This was the place that Pa had told them all about! This was the park!

"Hip, hip, roohay!" cried Max to the moon, and away he ran.

For the next few hours, he trotted busily about the park, shoving his snout into everything. Like most children, he was not only nosy but noisy too, and at the sound of his coming, the mice scuttled under the bandstand, the snakes slid away through the ornamental gardens, and the frogs plopped into the safe depths of the lily pond. Max caught nothing.

At last, he began to feel rather tired and to think how nice it would be to go home to bed. But which way was home?

Max considered this and came to the unhappy conclusion that he was lost. Just then, he saw, not far away, a hedgehog crossing the path, a large hedgehog, a Pa-sized hedgehog! What luck! Pa had crossed the street to find him! He ran forward, but when he reached the animal, he found it was a complete stranger.

"Oh," said Max. "I peg your bardon. I thought you were a different hodgeheg."

The stranger looked curiously at him. "Are you feeling all right?" he said.

"Yes, thanks," said Max. "Trouble is, I go to want home. But I won't know the day."

"You mean . . . you don't know the way?

"Yes."

"Well, where do you live?" asked the strange hedgehog.

"Number 5A."

"Indeed? Well now, listen carefully, young fellow. Go up this path—it will take you back to the street—and a little way along, you'll see a strange sort of house that humans use. It's a tall house, just big enough for one human to stand

59

up in, and it has windows on three sides and it's bright red. If you cross there, you'll come right to your own front gate, OK?"

"KO," said Max, "and thanks."

As soon as he went through the park railings, he saw the tall red house. He trotted up close to it. It was lit up, and sure enough, there was a human inside it. He was holding something to his ear, and Max could see that his lips were moving. How odd, thought Max, moving very close now, he's standing in there talking to himself!

At that instant, the man put down the receiver and pushed open the door of the telephone booth, a door designed to clear the pavement by about an inch, the perfect height for giving an inquisitive young hedgehog—for the second time in his short life—a tremendous bang on the head.

(continued on page 93)

Woolly

Snaggletooth was a caveman. He was short and strong and bowlegged and hairy, and he had a wife called Flatface.

Snaggletooth had several broken teeth that stuck out of his wide mouth, and his wife's face was indeed flat, and it isn't hard to guess why they called their small son Bat-ears.

One day Snaggletooth came rushing into their cave in high excitement.

"Guess what I've found, down by the river," he cried.

"Food, Snag?" said Flatface hopefully.

"Enough to last us for ages! A mammoth!"

"A mammoth? However will you be able to kill that?"

"I don't have to. It's dead already. Come on!" said Snaggletooth, and he hoisted Bat-ears onto his shoulders and set off back toward the river with Flatface following.

The huge animal was lying on its side, and while his parents stood gaping at the size of it, Bat-ears climbed up on top of it.

Behind it was a very sad-looking mammoth calf. Its tail hung down straight, its ears drooped, its head was bent, the eyes half-closed. It looked the picture of misery.

Oh dear, thought Bat-ears, this must be its mother who's died, and he slid down the far side of the body and stood before the youngster. It was not much taller than him.

"Hullo," he said. "I'm Bat-ears. What's your name?"

"Haven't got one," replied the little mammoth.

Bat-ears stroked the thick, sandy hair that covered the calf.

"You're woolly," he said, "so that's what I'll call you. Come and meet my mom and dad."

Snaggletooth and Flatface were surprised when Bat-ears appeared from behind the body followed by the calf.

Trustingly, it rested the tip of its trunk on his shoulder.

"Look!" he cried. "This is Woolly!" But at that very moment, they heard in the distance a horrible noise, a sort of mad, screeching laughter, and saw a crowd of ugly spotted shapes approaching at a gallop.

"Hyenas!" said Snaggletooth. "Quick, Bat-ears, jump on my back."

But Bat-ears was already mounted. He was sitting astride Woolly, legs tucked behind the young mammoth's ears, hands gripping the thick fleece.

"Go, Woolly, go!" he squeaked, and away they all went at top speed toward the river.

The river was a very big one, and out in the middle of it was a large island. Woolly pointed his little trunk at it.

"That's a nice place," he said to Bat-ears. "No hyenas. Plenty of good food."

"How do you know?"

"We used to go there."

"We? Oh, you mean you and your . . ."

". . . mother," said Woolly in a small voice.

"Oh. But how did you get there?"

"We swam."

"But none of us can swim."

"You don't have to," said Woolly. "I'll carry you, like I'm doing now. Your mom can ride behind you, and your dad can hang on to my tail."

"You can forget that," said Snaggletooth, who was frightened of the water. "There's no way I'm going in that water."

But then they heard the horrid laughter again. Some of the hyenas were coming down to the river to drink.

"Quick, Snag!" said Flatface, hastily clambering up behind Bat-ears.

"Quick, Dad!" cried Bat-ears.

"Quick!" trumpeted Woolly, and as the leading hyena dashed up, Snaggletooth threw himself desperately into the water. He grabbed hold of the young mammoth's tail, and away they went.

The island, they found, was a perfect paradise. It was covered with leafy trees, so there was plenty for Woolly to eat. And living on it were many small animals for the meat-eating cave-people to catch and many nestfuls of fat, white, sausage-shaped grubs whenever they just felt like a snack.

Soon the cave-people discovered how useful Woolly was to them. He found trees of crab apple and other wild fruit and broke off branches for them. He found bushes heavy with berries. He found patches of mushrooms, and dug up delicious truffles with his little tusks. He even found a wild bees' nest, and with his trunk, he pulled out the honeycomb for them. Never had they eaten so well.

"This is the life," said Snaggletooth, his mouth full of honey.

"Shall we stay here, Snag?" said Flatface.

"Can we, Dad?" said Bat-ears.

Snaggletooth had always lived in a cave.

"Where shall we sleep?" he said.

"Under the trees," said Flatface. "The weather's lovely and warm and settled, and there's masses of food."

"And we shan't be short of a drink," said Bat-ears.

The river, they soon found, was not just a protection against enemies. It was also full of fish, which Woolly caught for them.

He would dangle his trunk in the water, and when a fish swam up to investigate, he would suck so that the fish was drawn tight against the tip of his trunk. Then, with a swing of his head, he would flip it onto the bank.

He tossed frogs, too, with that trunk, and shook squirrels from bushes, and picked eggs from birds' nests.

"Woolly!" Flatface would say. "Whatever should we do without you!"

All the same, she worried about the approach of winter. What would they do when it got really cold, with no cave to shelter them? If only our people knew how to make fire, she thought—for once, when young, she had seen a forest ablaze, set off by a lightning strike, and she remembered the crackling of the flames, and the smoke, and, above all, the heat. There's plenty of deadwood on the island, she told herself, but no way to burn it.

She was wrong.

One day, they were all gathered around a tree that had fallen some long time ago by the look of it. It was partly hollow, and the wood inside it had decayed into a soft, dry powder—tinder, in fact.

Snaggletooth and Flatface were searching for grubs, and Woolly was stripping off and eating some of the remaining bark.

His appetite satisfied, he picked up a sharp piece of stick with his trunk and began to play with it, pushing it into the tinder and twiddling it to and fro, first one way, then the other, while Bat-ears watched idly. Held in that agile trunk tip, the stick rotated faster and faster, gradually drilling a hole in the tinder. And then suddenly a wisp of smoke came out of the hole!

"Look!" cried Bat-ears.

Snaggletooth and Flatface looked.

Woolly withdrew the stick.

Snaggletooth put his finger in the hole.

"Yeow!" he said. "Hot!"

Flatface grabbed a handful of dry grass.

"Go on, Woolly," she said.

Woolly twiddled some more.

"Faster! Faster!" cried Flatface, and as the smoke rose again, she began to feed the grass into the hole in the tinder.

"Twigs. Leaves. Anything dry, quick!" she said to the others. And then, as Woolly's wonderful trunk twiddled on, a tiny flicker was seen—the first little flame of the first fire ever lit on the face of Earth, not by nature, but by man.

Or rather, to be fair, by a mammoth.

Once they had become skilled in fire-making, something else happened that was to change their way of life. Until then, cave-people had always eaten their meat raw, just like the hyenas and the cave bears and the saber-toothed tigers. On the island, Snaggletooth and his family gobbled down the mice or squirrels or lizards they caught,

or the frogs and fish Woolly caught for them, not knowing there was a much tastier way of eating them. And once again, it was Woolly who made the breakthrough.

One evening, the family was sitting around a roaring fire (for the nights were growing colder) and eating a meal of fish Woolly had caught for them, when suddenly the mammoth picked up a fish with his trunk and dropped it into the hot embers at the edge of the blaze. The fish began to sizzle.

"Oh, Woolly," said Flatface. "Why did you do that? That's a fish wasted."

"Unless you can fish it out," said Snaggletooth. He laughed loudly at his own joke.

Woolly picked up a long stick, and with it, he moved the fish about so that first one side of it and then the other was exposed to the heat. All the while, the fish sizzled and hissed, and there arose from it a smell that was quite new to all of them, a delicious smell that made their mouths water.

Then Woolly flipped the fish onto the grass, and once it was cool enough, the cave-people each took a bite.

So it was that, thanks to a mammoth, Snaggletooth and his family became the first people on Earth not only to make fire but to discover cooking.

Not that they gave up eating meat raw on occasion, for their stomachs were strong and old habits die hard, and they would still pop such morsels as caterpillars into their mouths uncooked. But cooking, they found, made things so much nicer to eat, especially after Woolly had yet another brainwave.

One day, he came back from the river's edge, carrying something he had found there. It was the shell of a big turtle. The body had been eaten by ants and other scavengers, and only the deep basin-shaped shell was left. This, once Woolly had explained things to Flatface, became the world's first cooking utensil.

The shell, in which handfuls of fat, white grubs had been put, was laid in the fire, which quickly melted the grubs into a bubbling pool of fat. Into this fat were put not only the fish but also slivers of a large tuber-shaped vegetable that Woolly had dug up with his tusks and Flatface had sliced up with a sharp flint. So, once again thanks to the mammoth, there came about another first—fish and chips.

As the years passed, Woolly and his friends continued to live happily on the island in the middle of the great river. Snaggletooth had made a stone axe with which he chopped down trees and built a sort of house that the family could use for shelter from the occasional downpour (Woolly didn't mind the rain), and they always had plenty to eat.

In fact, Flatface became quite a good cook, inventing interesting recipes like boiled squirrel with frog sauce or fried snake garnished with green caterpillar dressing.

During all those years, Woolly grew big and Bat-ears grew tall and Snaggletooth grew fat.

Other cavemen living on either side of the river saw the smoke rising by day from the fires on the island and saw the flames of them by night. If the wind was in the right direction, they smelled delicious strange smells and heard voices and laughter and an occasional shrill trumpeting noise. They were scared, believing the island to be haunted, and none of them, even had it been possible, would have dared set foot there.

So, for the islanders, everything seemed to be perfect. But it wasn't quite, as Bat-ears and Woolly overheard one day.

They had been down to the river to bathe (something that Snaggletooth and Flatface never did; in fact, neither had ever in their whole lives even washed), and Bat-ears was riding home on his friend's great back. Woolly, now the owner of a magnificent pair of curving tusks, moved silently on his large cushioned feet. He stopped behind some bushes, close to the family house, to pull down the fruit with that long trunk of his. Bat-ears, a young man by now, slipped down to the ground, and at that moment heard his mother's voice.

"Snag," she was saying. "Are you happy?"

"Happy?" said Snaggletooth, rubbing his stomach, full as usual. "Of course I am. Aren't you?"

"Oh, yes," said Flatface, "except for one thing."

"What's that?"

Flatface did not answer for a moment, occupied as she was with tidying her matted gray locks with a comb made from an antelope's shoulder blade.

Then she said, "I just wish we could have had a grandchild. I'd love to have a little granddaughter, or a little grandson."

Her husband put his hand in his mouth and fingered one of his snaggle teeth. It was loose, because of his age, and now he pulled it out and threw it away.

"Grandchildren?" he said. "How's our Bat-ears going to manage that without a wife?"

This time Flatface made no answer, but the eavesdroppers could clearly hear the deep, sad sigh she gave.

Not only was each struck by the same thought but each knew what the other was thinking.

So it was that, one morning not long after, Snaggletooth and Flatface woke to find themselves alone on the island. Bat-ears and Woolly had disappeared!

They followed the mammoth's tracks, leading down to the river bank, but there was no sign of the pair. There was a message however. Drawn in the sand by the water's edge were two large arrows. One pointed to the distant shore, from which they had all come so many years ago. The other pointed the reverse way, inland toward their house.

"Oh, Snag!" cried Flatface, pointing to the first arrow. "They've gone and left us."

Snaggletooth pointed to the second arrow.

"But they'll come back," he said.

"When?"

"How do I know?"

In fact, months passed with no sign of them, until suddenly one day, the two old cave-people heard a loud shout coming from the direction of the river.

"Mom! Dad!" called Bat-ears over the wide waters. "We're back!"

And as they ran down to the bank, they saw the great head of Woolly approaching, trunk curled high out of the water, Bat-ears aboard.

But then their mouths fell agape in utter amazement. For sitting behind Bat-ears was another figure, the figure, they saw, of a towheaded cave-girl.

"Now," said Bat-ears when they had landed and the mammoth had shaken the water from his hairy sides, "let me introduce you. Mom, Dad, I want you to meet my girl-friend, Snubnose."

All that happened at the beginning of winter, and the following summer, would you believe, Snubnose had a little girl.

Bat-ears was the proudest of fathers, and Snaggletooth was quite pleased to be a grandfather, and Flatface was

utterly delighted with her granddaughter.

"She's got your ears," she said to her son, and to her daughter-in-law, "and your nose."

"And your face, Mom," said Bat-ears.

"But not your teeth, Snag," said Flatface.

Thank goodness, she thought.

All this time, Woolly stood silently by, his little, piggy eyes gazing affectionately down at the baby.

"What are you going to call her?" Snaggletooth asked the young couple.

"Well," said Snubnose, "Bat-ears wanted to name her

after his great friend, but 'Woolly' does sound a bit funny for a girl, doesn't it?"

"When she grows up," said Bat-ears, "we shall all tell her about the wonderful things her Uncle Woolly has done for us."

He looked up at the mammoth. "Perhaps you'd like to suggest a name?" he said.

Very gently, Woolly stretched out his trunk, and with the tip of it stroked the baby's head, already thickly covered with little ringlets. So fascinated was he that he hadn't been listening to what Bat-ears had said.

"She's lovely," he said dreamily.

"Oh, Woolly," said Bat-ears "I might have known you'd pick just the right name! We'll call her Lovely."

The Happiest Woodlouse

Walter was a wimp. He was scared of his own shadow—always had been since he was tiny. No matter that he was now a really big woodlouse, with fourteen strong legs and a fine coat of armor, Walter was still afraid of everything and anything. Spiders, black beetles, centipedes, earwigs—whatever kind of creature he met—frightened the life out of him so that he rolled himself into a ball and wouldn't unroll again for ages.

Even with other woodlice, he was just the same. Every time he met one, he rolled up and stayed rolled up until the patter of fourteen feet had died away in the distance.

You can easily understand why Walter had no friends.

I would like to make a friend, he said to himself. I would like to be able to have a good chat with someone, crack a joke or two perhaps. It must be nice to have a pal. If only I weren't so nervous.

At that moment, he heard someone approaching the large flat stone under which he was hiding, and hastily he curled himself into a ball. The footsteps came nearer, and suddenly, to his horror, Walter felt himself being nudged. It was the sort of hefty nudge, Walter thought, that some fierce creature might give a wretched woodlouse before picking it up and swallowing it whole.

But then he heard a voice. It was a jolly voice that did not sound fierce, but friendly.

"Wakey! Wakey!" said the voice. "What's a chap like you doing all curled up on a nice sunny day like this, eh?"

Could this be the friend I've been waiting for? thought Walter.

"What are you?" he said in somewhat muffled tones, for it is hard to speak clearly when you are curled up in a ball.

"I'm a woodlouse, of course, like you," said the voice. "Come on, unroll, why don't you? Anyone would think you were afraid of something."

If you only knew, said Walter to himself, I'm afraid of everything, but all the same, he unrolled to find himself face to face with a woodlouse of about his own size but of a slightly different color. Walter was slate gray. This stranger was paler, sort of brownish, in fact, and freckled all over.

Walter waved his antennae.

"Hullo," he said. "I'm Walter."

"Hi," said the stranger, waving back.

He looks a decent sort of chap, thought Walter. Well, it's now or never, so he took a deep breath and said, "Will you be my friend?"

"My!" said the freckly stranger. "You're a fast worker!"

"How do you mean?" said Walter.

"You don't waste time, do you? No remarks about the weather, no polite chitchat, just 'Will you be my friend?' Fairly takes a girl's breath away!"

A girl! thought Walter. I just wanted a pal to have a chat with and crack a joke to, but a girlfriend! Oh, no, I'm frightened of girls.

He was about to curl up again when the stranger said, "OK."

Walter hesitated.

"OK what?" he said.

"OK, I'll be your friend, Walter. I've seen worse-looking woodlice than you. By the way, my name's Marilyn."

"Oh," said Walter.

He wiggled several pairs of legs nervously.

"I'm pleased to meet you," he said.

"You're a funny boy," said Marilyn with a light laugh, and she moved forward until her antennae brushed gently against his.

At this touch, something like an electric shock ran through every plate of Walter's armor, and he found himself suddenly very short of breath.

"Come on," said Marilyn. "Let's go for a stroll."

Ordinarily Walter never came out from beneath his large flat stone until nightfall. Spiders and black beetles and centipedes and earwigs were frightening enough, but in daylight, out in the open, there was far worse danger. Birds! Birds with sharp eyes and sharper beaks that snapped up spiders and black beetles and centipedes and earwigs—and woodlice!

"Can't we wait until after dark, Marilyn?" he said.

Marilyn giggled.

"Oh, you are a one!" she said, and out she went, off along the garden path.

Despite himself, Walter followed. He was frightened, ter-
rified indeed, but he hurried after Marilyn as fast as his
seven pairs of legs could carry him. How beautiful she was,
he now could see. Her long antennae, the slender legs, each
delicate joint of her freckled carapace—all were perfection.

Here, in the wide open spaces of the garden, death might threaten, but without Marilyn, thought Walter, life would not be worth living.

"Wait for me!" he called. But even as he spoke, he saw, to his horror, that a huge, slimy monster squatted in the middle of the path ahead.

"Marilyn!" he cried. "Watch out!" And hastily he rolled himself into a ball. Miserably he waited, tightly curled. Cruel fate, thought Walter. I meet the love of my life, and

within minutes, she walks down a monster's throat. If only
I were brave, I might have tackled the brute. But I'm not,
alas, I'm not.

Then a voice said, "Are you coming, Walter, or aren't
you?"

"What were you playing at?" said Marilyn when, sheep-
ishly, he caught up with her. There was no sign of the monster except a trail of slime across the flagstones.

Walter gulped.

"I thought I saw a monster," he said.

"Monster?" said Marilyn. "That was only an old slug. Mind where you're putting your feet. The path's all sticky."

They walked on, off the path and onto a rose bed under whose bushes was a scattering of dead leaves. On these, they began to browse, side by side.

"Walter," said Marilyn.

"Yes, Marilyn?"

"You've got a yellow streak, haven't you?"

Walter did not answer.

"Not to mince words," said Marilyn, "you're a chicken-hearted scaredy-cat and a cowardy custard, aren't you?"

"Yes," said Walter.

"Well, at least you've been honest with me," said Marilyn, "so I'll do the same for you. Let's just forget the friendship bit. You're a nice boy, but if there's one thing I can't stand, it's a wimp. No hard feelings, eh?"

"But, Marilyn . . ." said Walter.

"Yes?"

"I . . . I love you."

For a moment, Marilyn gazed thoughtfully at Walter.

Such a good-looking fellow, but no backbone. Shame, really.

"Sorry, Walter," she said. "See you around, maybe." And she turned to go.

As she did so, Walter saw the thrush come hopping through the rose bed straight toward her.

Even as he tensed his muscles to roll himself into a ball, something snapped in his brain, and instead he rushed forward on his fourteen powerful legs.

"Roll up, quick!" he shouted at Marilyn, shoving her out of his way, and then, as instinctively she obeyed, Walter made directly for the huge bird.

"Take me!" he cried. "Take me, you brute, but spare my Marilyn!"

The thrush put its head on one side, the better to focus upon this foolhardy woodlouse, when it saw from the corner of its other eye a fat worm. Leaving Walter for dessert, it picked up the worm and swallowed it.

As it was doing so, a large tabby cat came strolling down the garden path, waving its tail, and the thrush flew hastily away.

"All clear!" cried Walter, and Marilyn unrolled.

"You saved my life!" she breathed.

"Well, I don't know about that," said Walter in an embarrassed voice.

"You jolly well tried to," said Marilyn. "You were ready to sacrifice yourself to protect me, weren't you?"

"Yes," said Walter.

Marilyn stared at her gallant knight in armor.

To think, she said to herself, that I called him a cowardy

custard. Her heart swelled within her bosom, and she went weak at the knees, all fourteen of them.

"Oh, Walter," she said softly, "I am yours, all yours."

"Oh, Marilyn," said Walter. "You have made me the happiest woodlouse in the world!"

The Coronation

from

A HODGEHEG STORY: KING MAX THE LAST

Max the hedgehog has been captured by two scientists who want to track his movements. Because a radio collar won't fit him, they decide to stick a transmitter on his spines. They add a little flashing light so they can spot him in the dark.

When a couple of days had gone by with no sight of Max, the family at Number 5A had almost given up hope of ever seeing him again. Ma was convinced he had been run over, even though Pa and Uncle B. had patrolled all the local roads and reported no squashings. Peony, Pansy, and Petunia, who were romantic girls, thought Max had fallen in love and was busy courting. They whispered and giggled a lot together.

(continued from page 60)

93

Pa decided that Max had simply left home to seek his fortune in the wide world.

"Didn't even bother to say goodbye," he grumbled.

Uncle B. said nothing, but he was sad, for he was especially fond of Max. He searched the park from end to end—in the ornamental gardens, around the bandstand, and beside the lily pond—and met a number of foraging hedgehogs but found no sign of his young friend.

Meanwhile the scientists' plans were going forward. They

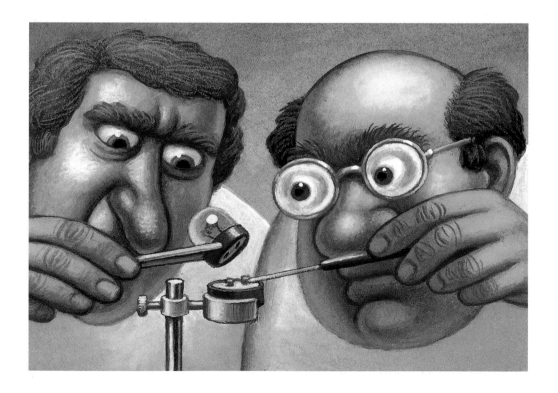

had prepared a very small battery-powered radio transmitter and had mounted on top of it a little electric lamp that revolved, like the beam of a lighthouse, throwing out a blue light.

Now all they had to do was to attach it to Max.

In fact, this turned out to be easy because, by now, Max had become used to them and no longer rolled up when handled.

They smeared superglue on the base of the transmitter and over the spines on the back of Max's neck, and managed, while Max was busy with his Munchimeat, to press the two surfaces together long enough for the glue to set.

"How about that?" said Dr. Dandy-Green.

"Just the job," said Professor Duck. "It looks as though he is wearing a crown."

"Other hedgehogs should be very impressed, especially when his little light is flashing," said Dr. Dandy-Green. "What with that and the transmitter, we'll be able to follow him wherever he goes."

As for Max, he hardly noticed the contrivance, for it weighed very little, and placed as it was, there was no way he could actually see it. All he thought about was freedom. Granted, he was well fed, but he was also fed up.

He would have been very happy if he could have understood what was said next.

"When shall we release him?" said Dr. Dandy-Green.

"Tomorrow evening?" said Professor Duck. "When we've tested the equipment?"

"OK. Where shall we release him?"

"In that park where we caught him, I should think. That's probably his home territory."

"He ought to have a name or a number or something," said the doctor.

"Yes," said the professor. "When we're writing up notes on his movements, we don't want to have to write 'the hedgehog did this or that' every time."

They looked at Victor Maximilian St. George, wearing (though he did not know it) his crown.

"We need something short," said Dr. Dandy-Green.

"How about 'E.E.'?" said Professor Duck.

"E.E.?"

"Yes. The initial of his Latin name, *Erinaceus Europaeus.*"

"E.E. it is!"

So the following day they tested the equipment, allowing Max to trot around the laboratory floor and up and down the corridors, while they took turns in holding the receiver and following him about. All worked perfectly. The transmitter transmitted, the receiver received, and the flashing light flashed.

The last thing puzzled Max since he could not see where the intermittent blue light was coming from, but he soon grew used to it. He was disappointed to be put back into his cage, but then, that evening, he left it for good.

What happened next is best described by the notes that Professor Duck and Dr. Dandy-Green wrote up the following day.

10:30 P.M. Took E.E. to park, released beside bandstand. E.E. raised snout, scented air, set off NNW across park toward nearest road (B 7216), traveling fast. This route involved skirting lily pond and cutting through ornamental gardens, where it was not easy to observe light in dense shrubbery, flower beds, etc., and radio contact was needed. In open ground, E.E.'s light easily visible. Nervous moments on E.E.'s arrival at road since evening traffic still moderately busy. Astonished to observe E.E. waiting patiently at curbside until road was quite clear. E.E. then looked left, looked right, looked left again, and calmly crossed, revolving light flashing. Fortunately, this phenomenon was observed by Prof. D. and Dr. D.-G. only. E.E. then went under a gate (Number 5A) and into a suburban garden. Looking over garden wall, Prof. D. and Dr. D.-G. saw several hedgehogs that all fled at E.E.'s approach. Continued observation, however, revealed that these animals (two adults and three juveniles) returned cautiously after a while and were then joined by another adult from the garden of Number 5B. Much squeaking, grunting, and cough-like snorts ensued. Waited some time, but E.E. seemed unwilling to move further, so discontinued observation at 11:43 P.M.

The family at Number 5A had been quietly snail hunting in the rock garden, when suddenly, under the gate, had come the strangest apparition. It looked like Max, it smelled like Max, but what was that strange object on its head, and what was that ghastly blue light that flickered round and round and lit them up in turn? For an instant, they froze in terror, and then Ma squealed, "It's his ghost! It's our Max's ghost, come to haunt us!" and they all scurried for cover.

Max stood in the middle of the lawn and called, "Ma! Pa! Girls! It's only me. I'm home."

Pa was first out of the flower bed. He approached Max cautiously, blinking each time the flashes passed over him.

"Is it really you, son?" he said.

"Yes, Pa."

"What's that thing on your head?"

"I can't see it, Pa," Max said.

Peony, Pansy, and Petunia came forward.

"Oo!" they squeaked. "Look at Max's hat! Isn't it pretty! Can we have hats like that, Ma?"

Ma shuffled nervously nearer.

"Oh, Max!" she said. "Whatever's happened to you?"

Max was about the tell them all about being captured by the two men and put in a cage, but just then Uncle B. came pushing through the hedge. He saw Max and stopped dead in his tracks.

"Oh no!" he said softly. "It cannot be!"

"It is!" the others cried. "It's our Max!"

"But can't you see what he is wearing?" said Uncle B. "Have you never heard of the legend of the King?"

"What king?" they said.

"Why!" cried Uncle B. "The King of the Hedgehogs! See his crown of light! Your boy Max has been chosen to rule over hedgehogkind!"

Have I? thought Max. King of the Hedgehogs, eh? Sounds a bit of all right, that does.

He lowered his head so that the blue light shone more brightly upon them all.

"Bless you, my people," he said.

The Excitement of Being Ernest

The first thing that struck you about Ernest was his color. If you had to give a name to it, you would say "honey"—not the pale wax honey that needs a knife to get it out of a jar, but the darker, richer, runny stuff that drips all over the tablecloth if you don't twist the spoon around in it properly.

That was the color of Ernest's coat. And the second thing about him that was remarkable was the amount of coat he carried. He was very hairy. Body, legs, tail, all had their fair share of that runny-honey-colored hair, but it

was Ernest's face that was his fortune, with its fine beard and moustaches framed by shortish, droopy ears. From under bushy eyebrows, Ernest looked out upon the world and found it good. Only one thing bothered him. He did not know what kind of dog he was.

It should have been simple, of course, to find out. There were a number of other dogs living in the village who could presumably have told him, but somehow Ernest had never summoned the courage to ask. To begin with, the other dogs all looked so posh. They were all of different breeds, but each one appeared so obviously well-bred, so self-assured, so upper class, that Ernest had always hesitated to approach them, least of all with a daft question like, "Excuse me. I wonder if you could tell me what sort of dog I am?"

For that matter, he thought to himself one day, I don't even know what sort of dogs they are, and then it occurred to him that would be a much more sensible question to ask and could lead perhaps to the kind of conversation about breeds in general where one of them might say, "I'm a Thingummytite, and you, I see, are a Wotchermecallum."

So after he had helped to get the cows in for morning

105

milking on the farm where he lived, Ernest trotted up to the village to the gateway of the manor house—an imposing entrance flanked by fine pillars—and peered in from under his bushy eyebrows. Standing in the driveway was the manor house dog. Ernest lifted his leg politely on one of the fine stone pillars and called out, "Excuse me! I wonder if you could tell me what sort of dog you are?"

"Ich bin ein German shorthaired pointer," said the manor house dog, "if dot is any business of yours."

"Oh," said Ernest. "I'm not one of those."

He waited expectantly to be told what he was.

"Dot," said the German shorthaired pointer pointedly, "is as plain as der nose on your face," and he turned his back and walked away.

Ernest went on to the vicarage, and saw, through the front gate, the vicar's dog lying on the lawn.

"Excuse me," said Ernest, lifting his leg politely on the gate. "I wonder if you could tell me what sort of dog you are?"

"Nom d'un chien!" said the vicar's dog. "Je suis un French bulldog."

"Oh," said Ernest. "I'm not one of those."

The French bulldog snorted, and though Ernest waited hopefully for a while, it said nothing more, so he walked down the road until he came to the pub.

The pub owner's dog was very large indeed, and Ernest thought it best to keep some distance away. He lifted his leg

discreetly on an empty beer keg and shouted across the pub parking lot, "Excuse me! I wonder if you could tell me what sort of dog you are?"

"Oi'm an Irish wolf-hound," said the pub owner's dog in a deep, rumbly voice.

"Oh," said Ernest. "I'm not one of those."

"Bedad you're not," said the Irish wolfhound. "Shall Oi be after tellin' yez what sort of a dog ye are?"

"Oh, yes please," said Ernest eagerly.

"Sure ye're a misbegotten hairy mess," said the Irish wolfhound, "and it's stinking of cow muck ye are. Now bate it, if ye know what's good for you."

Ernest beat it. But he wasn't beaten.

He paid a call on a number of houses in the village street, repeating his polite inquiry and receiving answers of varying degrees of rudeness from a Tibetan terrier, an American cocker spaniel, a Finnish spitz, and a Chinese crested dog. But none of them volunteered any information about what kind of animal he was.

There was one house left, by the junction of the road and the lane that led back to the farm. Standing outside it was a dog that Ernest had never seen before in the neighborhood. It looked friendly and wagged its long, plumy tail as Ernest left his customary calling card on the gate.

"Hullo," he said. "I haven't seen you before."

"We've just moved in," said the friendly stranger. "You're the first dog I've met here, actually. Are there a lot in the village?"

"Yes."

"Decent bunch?

Ernest considered how best to answer this.

"They're all very well-bred," he said. "I imagine they've got pedigrees as long as your tail," he added, "like you have, I suppose?"

"Well, yes, you could say that," replied the other. "For what it's worth."

Ernest sighed. I'll give it one more go, he thought.

"Straight question," he said. "What sort of dog are you?"

"Straight answer, English setter—well, at least on my mother's side."

"English?" said Ernest delightedly. "That's a change."

"How do you mean?"

"Why, the rest of them are Chinese, German, Tibetan, Irish, American, Finnish—there's no end to the list."

"Really? No, no, I'm as English as you are."

"Ah," said Ernest carefully. "Then you know what sort of dog I am?"

"Of course," said the setter. "You're a Gloucestershire cow dog."

The hair over Ernest's face prevented the setter from seeing the changing expression that flitted across it, first of astonishment, then of excitement, and finally a studied look of smug satisfaction.

"Ah," said Ernest. "You knew. Not many do."

"My dear chap," said the setter. "You amaze me. I should have thought that any dog would have recognized a Gloucestershire cow dog immediately."

"Really?" said Ernest. "Well, I suppose any English dog would."

"Yes, that must be it. Anyway, you'll be able to compete with all these pedigree chaps next week."

"Why, what's happening next week?"

"It's the village fête."

"Oh, I don't go to that sort of thing," said Ernest. "I've got too much work to do with the cows."

"Quite. But this year, there's a new attraction, apparently. They've just put the posters up, haven't you seen?"

"Didn't notice," said Ernest.

"Well, there's one stuck on our wall. Come and have a look."

And this is what they saw.

VILLAGE FÊTE
SATURDAY JUNE 15th
BY KIND PERMISSION
IN THE GROUNDS OF THE
MANOR HOUSE

Skittle Alley

Coconut Shy

Cake Stall

Jam and Preserve Stall

White Elephant Stall

Hoopla

Wellie-throwing Competition

Guess the Weight of the Pig

Grand Dog Show

"But that's no good," said Ernest. "With all the pedigree dogs in the village, the judge will never look at me twice."

"But that's no good," said Sally. "With all the pedigree dogs

in the village, the judge will never look at Ernest twice." Sally was the farmer's daughter, and she was looking at another of the notices, tacked on the farm gate.

"Oh, I don't know," said her father. "You might be surprised. Have a go. It's only a bit of fun. You'll have to clean him up a bit, mind."

So when the great day dawned, Ernest ran to Sally's whistle after morning milking and found himself, to his surprise and disgust, required to stand in an old tin bath and

be soaked and lathered and scrubbed and hosed, and then blow-dried with Sally's mother's hair dryer plugged into an electric outlet in the barn.

"He looks a treat," said the farmer and his wife when Sally had finished combing out that long, honey-colored coat. And he did.

Indeed, when they all arrived at the fête, a number of people had difficulty in recognizing Ernest without his usual covering of cow muck. But the dogs weren't fooled.

Ernest heard them talking among themselves as the competitors began to gather for the dog show, and their comments made his head drop and his tail droop.

"Well, I'll be goshdarned!" said the American cocker spaniel to the Tibetan terrier. "Will ya look at that mutt! Kinda tough to have to share a show ring with no-account trash like that."

And, turning to the Finnish spitz, "Velly distlessing," said the Chinese crested dog. "No pediglee."

"Ma foi!" said the French bulldog to the Irish wolfhound. "Regardez zis 'airy creature! 'E is, 'ow you say, mongrel?"

"Begorrah, it's the truth ye're spakin," said the Irish wolfhound in his deep rumbly voice, "and it's stinking of soap powder he is."

As for the German shorthaired pointer, he made sure, seeing that he was host for the day, that his comment on Ernest's arrival on the croquet lawn (which was the show ring) was heard by all.

"Velcome to der manor, ladies and gentlemen," he said to the other dogs. "May der best bred dog vin," and he

turned his back on Ernest in a very pointed way.

"Don't let them get you down, old chap," said a voice in Ernest's ear, and there, standing next to him, was the friendly setter, long, plumy tail wagging.

"Oh, hullo," said Ernest in a doleful voice. "Nice to see you. I hope you win, anyway. I haven't got a chance."

"Oh, I don't know," said the setter. "You might be surprised. Have a go. It's only a bit of fun." He lowered his voice. "Take a tip though, old chap. Don't lift your leg. It's not done."

Suddenly Ernest felt much happier. He gave himself a good shake, and then, when they all began to parade around the ring, he stepped out smartly at Sally's side, his long, (clean) honey-colored coat shining in the summer sunshine.

The judge examined each entry in turn, looking in their mouths, feeling their legs and their backs, studying them from all angles, and making them walk up and down, just as though it were a class in a championship show.

When her turn came, he said to Sally, "What's your dog called?"

"Ernest."

From under bushy eyebrows, Ernest looked out upon the judge.

"Hullo, Ernest," the judge said, and then hesitated, because there was one thing that bothered him. He did not know what kind of dog Ernest was.

"You don't see many of these," he said to Sally.

"Oh yes you do. There are lots about."

"Lots of . . . ?"

"Gloucestershire cow dogs."

"Of course, of course," said the judge.

When he had carefully examined all the entries, he made them walk around once more, and then he called out the lady of the manor with her German shorthaired pointer. When they came eagerly forward, trying not to look too smug, he said, "I've finished with you, thank you."

And he called out, one after another, the Chinese crested dog and the Tibetan terrier and the American cocker spaniel and the French bulldog and the Irish wolfhound and, to finish with, the Finnish spitz, and said to each in turn, "I've finished with you, thank you."

Until the only dogs left on the croquet lawn were the setter and Ernest.

And the judge looked thoughtfully at both of them for quite a time before he straightened up and spoke to the owner of the setter.

"A very close thing," he said, "but I'm giving the first prize to the Gloucestershire cow dog," and he walked across to the vicar, whose job it was to make all the announcements on the public address system.

"Well done, old boy," said the setter. "It couldn't have happened to a nicer chap."

"But I don't understand," said Ernest. "How could I have won? Against all you aristocratic fellows that are registered with the kennel club, and have lots of champions in your pedigrees?"

"Listen," said the setter as the loudspeaker began to crackle and the voice of the vicar boomed across the gardens of the manor house.

"Ladies and gentlemen! We have the result of our grand dog show! It's not quite like Westminster, ha, ha—we do things a bit differently down here—and in our show there has been only one class, for the most lovable dog. And the winner is . . . Ernest, the Gloucestershire cow dog!"

And Sally gave Ernest a big hug, and the judge gave Sally a little cup, and the setter wagged his plumy tail like mad,

and everybody clapped, and Ernest barked and barked so loudly that he must have been heard by nearly every cow in Gloucestershire.

Oh, the excitement of being Ernest!

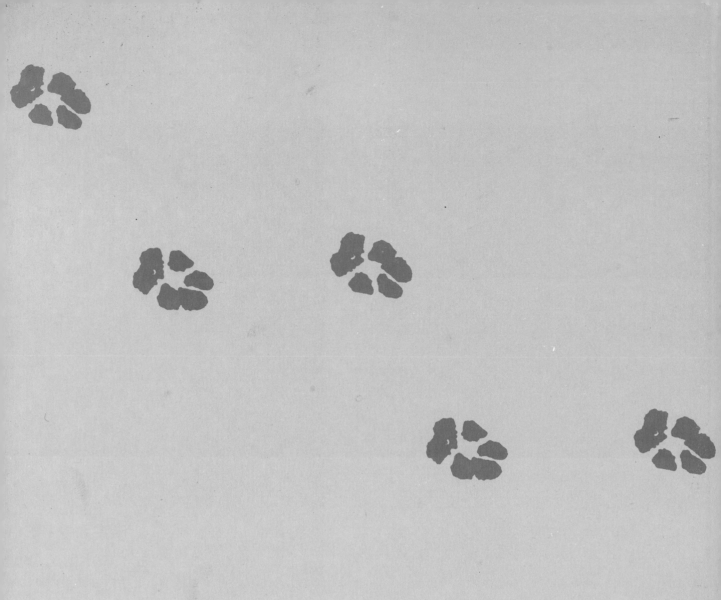